Easy
Jobs

By Keith Hedger

To my wife Terri: your support and encouragement are a big part of why this story exists. Thank you. Love you always.

Chapter 1

Hitcher sucked air through his teeth as he watched his electronic lock-pick. Voices cursing in Spanish jerked his head back down the hallway and his hand under his jacket. A green LED brought his attention back and relaxed his hand. He pushed the door open and stepped into humid August air. He snagged the pick on the way through.

"Jacket might have been too much," Hitcher said.

The twenty meter gap between the door and the compound wall lit up like it was noon. Hitcher's cybereyes cycled until they filtered out enough light for him to function. He sprinted, pushing his body across the gap to the wall. Traces of bright red flashed past him, his cybereyes translating the heat from bullets to streaks in his vision. Gasping in wet air, he forced himself to run faster.

He jumped from three steps away, gloved hand stretching for the top of the wall. Glass tinkled as his weight smashed through his glove's reinforced palm onto the shards cemented into the top of the wall. His feet scrambled against the brick, and a heartbeat later he passed over the wall. Something tugged at his jacket as he went over. Pain shot through his fingers as glass sliced skin. He dropped two meters back to the ground on the far side of the wall, rolling across the dirt.

His vision shifted to the low light spectrum, countering the park's sudden darkness, by the time he reached his feet. Fewer shots rang out. He pulled close to a clump of bushes and trees for cover. Hitcher's eyes picked up three heat signatures at the last second. Security troops, two lifting weapons and one moving to block him.

Hitcher held his pace, reached out with one hand and punched the closest troop in the chest. The man's weapon dropped as the air rushed out of him. Another step and he back handed the next guard, sending the man spinning away. Rolling with the momentum from the slap, Hitcher's shoulder dropped. When he slammed into the last security guy, it reminded Hitcher of a very surprised quarterback he had tackled during a high school football game a decade before.

Checking the park surrounding the embassy his cybereyes gauged the distance to the road at two hundred meters. His legs and lungs burned from the short stretch he had covered. Scanning ahead, he spotted more likely ambush sites. He angled toward the first area, a thicket of bushes. Nothing hid on the other side as the leaves brushed against his jacket. Hitcher made a lot of noise, and he knew it, but with the distance left to cover, stealth was no longer a factor in his escape.

Blasting through the thicket, Hitcher caught a bit of movement against the distant lights. He ducked under the stun bar swinging at him. His pistol angled toward the man and fired twice. The security guy slammed back into a tree with a grunt. His friends came in fast, jabbing their stunners at Hitcher's head.

Shifting and twisting, Hitcher caught one stick near the hand grip. The security troop's face shield ripped away as Hitcher's pistol tore it off. The impact broke the connection to the gun camera, cutting the targeting caret out of his vision. Turning toward the last security trooper, he shoved the pistol into the troop's face shield. Stepping forward drove his weight into the strike. Bone crunched as the shield hammered into the troop's nose. Blood covered the bottom of the mask.

Getting his pistol settled back into his hand, the caret returned to his vision. He judged the distance at a hundred meters. In his military days, that was fifteen seconds if he was feeling slow. Gasping air into his burning lungs, he reminded himself that it had been a couple of years since he ran like that. Adding in boots, jeans, and an armored jacket, doing the hundred in a minute would be impressive.

His mistake occurred to him a half second too late. He crossed too far from the next thicket. A blur of motion slammed into him, driving him into a tree. Reacting, he drove his elbow into the attacker. His elbow flared as it impacted on the helmet, but the attacker backed off. Striking again, he turned, getting his pistol into the fight. The security trooper shook off the hit and turned to face him.

The pistol barked twice. Hitcher realized what happened before the second round fired but training and instinct were running the show. Conscious thought came in a light second behind. The first round found a flaw in the face shield's material, sending spiderwebs across it. His second round shattered it. The face behind the shield erupted blood and bone. A heartbeat later the body collapsed. Hitcher gazed at the corpse. His training had created a big problem for him.

"Mother fuck," he grunted.

He ran again. The Thursday night traffic was light as he crossed the street. Checking the streets, Hitcher decided on a route that would sink him deep into the warehouses and old factory buildings in the area. Sweat made his t-shirt and jacket stick to his skin. Finally, he noticed the staring crowd and slowed to a walk. Many of the places were clubs, with a noticeable population of toughs who were eyeing him and his pistol.

Gasping from the run, Hitcher tucked his still warm pistol into his waistband. A quick tug hid the pistol under his jacket. A few of those watching shrugged it off. He was no longer a threat. Others continued checking him, though. There was a call he had to make and dodging crowds while he talked would make it more complicated. Turning down an alley, he opened his implanted phone.

Chapter 2

"We have something, Comandante," A young man spoke from a security station.

"What?" the security officer asked, crossing the room in two strides.

"Sergeant Gonzalez's camera got a feed," he replied, "I don't think Sergeant Gonzalez survived."

"She didn't," the officer confirmed, "They're returning her body. Show me the feed."

The analyst clicked on the video file Gonzalez's camera had delivered to the embassy's servers. The wireless access points hidden throughout the park surrounding the compound were useful for many things. Returning data from security assets, such as the late Sergeant Gonzalez's camera feed, was a primary use. Allowing easy connection to mobile phones had also proven to be of great benefit. The Holy Mexican Empire's embassy in Atlanta had gained a great deal of data about those passing through, building extensive dossiers on regular visitors.

The image was moving and grainy with grayish greens from the camera's low light mode. It was only a couple of seconds before two bright flashes. A few seconds of bouncing grays and greens passed, and the video settled on a series of flashing lights in the distance.

"That's not much," the officer said.

"I can pass the footage through some filters, Comandante," the analyst said, "We got a shot of the infiltrator escaping. With a little time, we can get a height and weight estimate. With a little work, a rough face to identify."

"How much time?"

"I should be able to clean up the facial information in a few minutes. Enough to get a rough sketch, at least, Comandante."

"Get me that sketch," the officer said, "I will see about getting some dogs to hunt our fox. I'll also inform the Bishop of the infiltration."

"Yes, Comandante," Jaime said.

"Young man, I hope your skills are as good as you think. The Bishop does not like to be disappointed." the commander focused on the analyst, "Neither do I."

"Yes, Comandante."

Chapter 3

"Call Micky," Hitcher murmured, triggering his phone implant. The ringing indicator centered in his left eye and then slid down to the corner of his field of vision. Walking as he waited for an answer, Hitcher stepped out of the alley and turned onto the sidewalk. Several people chilled, a few using old fashioned cellular phones.

Scanning the crowds, he noted one guy looking him over. His eyes glazed over for a second. Hitcher turned and crossed the street while the phone indicator continued to ring. Once he crossed the street, he glanced back. His watcher seemed uninterested. Breathing deep, he ducked into a shop, exiting through a side door.

"Come on, man," Hitcher whispered while the phone rang, "I don't need your fuckin' voice mail."

On the seventh ring, Micky answered.

"Took you long enough, geek," Hitcher sub vocalized.

"Yeah, and she was all happy, too," Micky replied, "You good?"

"I don't know," Hitcher said, "Had to mix it up with some folks on the way out."

"Bad?"

"Real sure I killed a security guard."

"But you got the prize?"

"Yeah, I got the prize. Gut says they're looking for me, though."

"What's your plan?"

"Don't know. I'm a long way from a ride so I don't know whether to hole up or run for it."

"Hang on, checking the boards."

Hitcher wanted to do anything except hang on. However, he kept moving, eyes roving across the people out for their evening debauchery. He towered over most of the partiers. Slumping his shoulders and keep his eyes angled down were the best he could do to avoid attracting attention.

"Someone's trying to hire every merc in the area," Micky said.

"How much?"

"More than I'd pay for you," Micky said, "Real good for a quick 'find a guy that looks like this' gig."

"Not making me feel better."

"Call mommy to feel better," Micky suggested. "Yeah, looks like it's the Mexicans funding it. Just basing that on a couple of freelance talent scouts they use a lot. And, yes, it does look like you're in the middle of a potential ground zero."

"How do I get out?"

"Keep your head low. You interested in some work up north?"

"Will it get me out of here faster?"

"Yeah, it will. Besides, I need the prize. So I'm going to get someone to get you out. Then I'll see if I can get Burn and Karma to get you up north. Sound good?"

"I get paid?"

"You get paid and you get out of Atlanta for a while," Micky said.

"I'm in."

"Great. Right now, keep moving, try to keep out of sight, and I'll get help headed to you. Keep the line clear, Hitcher. And last, don't let yourself get backed into a corner. I can't get an army to pull you out, and I'd rather not see Burn and Karma do any form of urban redevelopment."

"Got it. Keep low and stay to the shadows. Who is Burnin' Karma?"

"Do that. It's Burn and Karma. Two people. Call you in a bit," Micky said before cutting the call.

"You do that, man. You fuckin' hurry."

Chapter 4

Karma's head snapped left when she heard a pistol fire. Burn's gun based on the angle. A guy collapsed to the floor, a revolver tumbling out of his hand to rest a few centimeters away. Brain matter splattered the window, and blood pooled from the exit wound. Taking a deep breath, she turned to the storage box on the table.

"That," she said, "was not in the plan."

She pushed her lock breaker drive into the slot on the container. The red LED indicator shone balefully in the dim light.

"Wasn't supposed to be anyone here," Burn said.

"I remember that. Out at the club with his boyfriend," Karma said, staring at the red light.

Burn's footsteps were just loud enough for Karma to track her movements. Four steps before Burn stopped.

"No one else back there. He's not the guy from the pictures, either."

"Easy job. Go in, get the prototype, walk out the condo doors."

"No one hires us for easy jobs," Burn replied. "Let's hope it doesn't get worse."

The red light died. Karma felt her heart beat once. It lit green, glaring in the darkness. The lid of the container slid back, allowing her to see the odd little chip seated in a padded case. Taking a deep breath, Karma reached in. With a gentle touch, she lifted the chip container and tucked it into an inside pocket of her jacket. Finally, she exhaled the breath she had been unconsciously holding.

As she pulled the lock pick out of the slot a screeching siren went off, accompanied with red flashing strobe lights.

"That was not in the plan," popped in the text message box in Karma's vision.

"No shit," Karma replied. *"Is it just noise and light?"*

"Building security is deploying. No chemical systems this high up, though."

"So much for using the elevator. Get your harness ready."

"We're a hundred and ten floors up," Burn sent back. *"Fuck. Security troops blocking stairs, and the elevators are locked down. Wait, one coming up. Camera shows a security team."*

"Fight through 'em?"

"Heavy squad. Someone's pissed."

"Gonna have to go at the same time. You want to handle the rappel?" Karma moved her hands around, getting gear ready.

"I'll shoot, you handle the rappel. You good with this?"

"Face to face, I'm going Aussie," Karma said. *"Time to clip on."*

Karma placed the magnetic base of a spool of cable against the steel post framing the condo's floor to ceiling window. Burn stepped in front of her and began connecting clips from her tactical harness to the one Karma wore. When Karma signaled she was ready, Burn jumped up, wrapping her legs around Karma's waist. In a blur, she drew both of her pistols, and tucked her head down, pressing her eyes into Karma's shoulder.

A pistol fired repeatedly. Burn heard the cracking sound as the window punctured and felt Karma push them forward. Her back hammered into the clear flexible plastic window. The window gave a second of resistance and then cracked and shattered away from Burn's back. Everything shifted. A wave of nausea flashed through Burn as her body leveled and the feed from the gun cameras disrupted her brain's ability to adjust. The rush of air past Burn's head drown out all sound.

"How long is the cable?" Burn messaged.

"Fifty meters. Got a second spool."

"That's going to leave us short."

"Don't distract me. Gotta plant the second spool, or we'll find out what deceleration trauma is like," Karma replied.

"Watching for threats."

Burn checked the condo window, watching for the security team that should be hitting the condo any second. The links to her pistols fed her data, including the fact that she was a round short in her right hand pistol. She wondered if the corpse on the floor would slow the security team down at all. A half second later, her cybereyes magnified a shape sticking out of the window. It was a security troop's helmet and one arm, pointing a rifle at them. Clearly the corpse was not a shock.

"Incoming fire," Burn sent the message as she raised her pistols. The sights stabilized, adjusted for distance, and settled in.

She fired off three rounds from each pistol. The security shooter was not in great danger. Burn knew that, but the threat put his own shots far wide of them. That was worth the effort, she decided. Before the shooter could settle down she fired two more rounds at him.

"You know this is insane, right?" Burn messaged.

"Seventy meters left," came Karma's reply as she reached behind her, *"Troops on the ground. We're gonna have to drop more than I figured."*

"How far?"

"Fifteen meters, maybe," Karma replied, *"Sixty meters, spool off."*

Burn watched the second spool sail off toward a support frame. As it flew, the end of the first spool hung in the air. Holding her breath, Burn focused on the spool, willing it to reach the support. The magnetic base struck and stuck.

"Fucking close," Burn muttered.

"Hang on," Karma said, kicking off to push them left, *"Might be a twenty meter drop."*

"Long drop."

"Shouldn't reach terminal velocity. I think."

"You should have paid attention in physics class," Burn said.

"Don't remember taking physics class. Shooters below."

Burn's cybereyes converted the heat trails of the rounds flying up past them to red streaks.

"Not an easy job," Burn said, *"How long?"*

"Five seconds," Karma sent, *"I've got the low clips."*

Burn holstered her pistols and placed her fingers on the clips connecting them at the shoulders.

"Go."

"Unclip in two. One. Now!"

Burn unclipped and then felt Karma push her away. After that, she focused on the sidewalk rushing toward her. Something flashed through her vision, rocketing toward a group of security troops on the sidewalk. A new message from Karma popped up.

"Fire in the hole."

'The fuck?" Burn said aloud.

The grenades detonated. They were fragmentation grenades, but the concussion from the devices was more helpful. Red heat trails bounced from the troops' armor causing the troops to tumble to the ground and clutch their ears. Burn focused again on the sidewalk, bending her knees a little, and preparing for impact.

Her feet stung as her boot heels touched the concrete. Burn rolled to her left and back, burning off the excess energy from the drop. Coming back to her feet, she stumbled until she slammed into the building. Targeting data was feeding to her from the pistol she had drawn, though.

"Moving west," Karma said.

Burn joined her partner, running hard and covering the security team as they tried to get to their feet. With weapons scattered, they tried to cover their own and get organized. Burn and Karma kept moving. Karma turned to check their rear.

Burn had an incoming call. A hacker buddy of theirs who sometimes had work for them. She twitched her tongue against an incisor, which caused the system to send the call to voice mail. Her vision cleared of the call indicator, and she focused on reaching the end of the block. Karma fired a couple of shots behind them.

"*Whenever someone says it's an 'easy job',*" Karma texted, "*I'm bringing the fucking H&K.*"

"*A little bit of overkill.*"

"*As long as the threats are killed. Right at the corner. Cross the street.*"

They turned, crouching, and crossed the street. Burn's sight feed showed a handful of security people running toward them. Not fast or well, but a few were chasing them. Karma sent half a dozen more rounds their way. Burn added a few for good measure. It would be a miracle to hit anyone, but the fire made them dodge and look for cover.

"*Car ahead,*" Karma said.

"*The one the guy's next too?*"

"*That's our ride,*" Karma confirmed, lifting her pistol, "Hey!"

The man turned toward them. His hair showed touches of gray in the street lights, and his car was a new sedan. Cybereyes dialed in to check his left hand. No ring, but a tan line from one. Middle class corporate manager out to party after the divorce, Burn guessed. If she were wrong, it would not make a big difference.

"Gimme the keys." Karma ordered, coming around the car, her pistol trained on him, "Now."

"I just bought this," he complained, holding out the keys.

"You'll get it back in a week or so," Karma took the keys, thumbing the unlock button on the chip, "Or the insurance company will cover you. Forget you saw us."

"Forget hot girls like you? Especially when

you're stealing my car."

"Might get a date," Burn said, "If you're really confused about what the thief looked like."

"Hispanic male, just under two meters," the guy offered.

"Good enough," Karma said as she dropped into the driver seat, "See you later."

"He must be a veteran," Burn said as she climbed into the passenger seat.

He stumbled away from the car as Karma cut it out of the parking space and onto the street. Burn checked the mirror on her side of the car. The security people were just catching up to the guy. She checked her messages again. Micky had texted her.

"Have a job. Still busy? Let Karma up for air and call me."

She chuckled, and replied, "Still busy. Car chase. Send details. And don't be an asshole."

The reply came a few seconds later.

"Easy job. Escort a guy to Pittsburgh."

"Where we going?" Burn spoke.

"The meet to drop the prize," Karma said, "That's the plan."

"Micky has a job. Says it's an easy job."

Karma pulled a hard right turn, causing the tires to squeal and jump.

"What're you doing?"

"Getting my H&K. Reschedule the drop and get the details on Micky's job. And tell him he's an asshole."

"I already told him that. And getting the H&K is definitely not on the plan."

"New plan."

"Gotcha, babe."

Chapter 5

Setting the top button of her suit jacket, Sarra checked her appearance in her mirror.

"Just right," she said, shifting so her cleavage settled to her satisfaction.

The call indicator came up in the lower corner of her left eye. It identified the caller as Micky.

"Son of a bitch," she said before opening the call, "Hello, Micky. Looking for a date?"

"Love to, Sarra, but I've got things going on," Micky replied, "I do have a date for you though."

"I can find my own hook ups, baby. Why should I meet your friend?"

"Because he needs a friend and a place to hang for a couple of hours. And you, my lovely lady, are very good at being a friend and you know all the best places to lay low."

"I need details, Micky," she said. "You know, I might actually have plans this evening. This is going to cost you."

"Oh, I'm sure of that. It's a guy named Hitcher. I need him in Pittsburgh, and it seems the Mexicans want him. A lot. Not even pretending this is a safe job."

"Where do I pick him up?"

"He's in the strip over near the Mexican embassy. He's trying to stay out of sight, and they're hiring everyone they can to find him. Think you can link up and get him out of there?"

"I can. Probably. If he can keep out of trouble until I get there."

"Okay, how much?"

"How long do I have to baby sit?"

"Two hours. Three max."

She gave Micky a number that was triple her usual rate for short term jobs.

"Done. Here's his current location and number. You got a clean number to use?"

"Yes. Why aren't you coordinating this?"

"Because I'm also working on getting the transport team lined up. Give me fifteen minutes and make contact if I haven't contacted you."

"I'll be rolling in fifteen," Shawna said, "You get thirty minutes to get in contact. I'll try to reach your boy twice after that. If he's too deep in, you might have to write him off. I'm not equipped for high threat response work, love."

"If it's that deep, I'll make sure he knows to run and gun. You get moving. I've got another call to make."

"It's always a pleasure doing business with you, Micky. Now, how about one of these Friday nights, we make a business of doing some pleasure?"

"I keep trying, babe, but I'm growing convinced that the universe just doesn't want us together."

"You keep blaming the universe but I think you're scared of me. Later."

Sarra stepped back in front of the mirror. After a moment, she walked to her night stand and pulled out a heavy semiautomatic. Tucking the pistol into her purse, she smiled.

"A girl should always accessorize appropriately for her activities."

Chapter 6

Burn took Micky's call on the second ring. The sedan had a surprisingly high end sound system, and Karma dialed a pirate station running through a mix of kill metal and viking rap. Based on her driving being smoother with the music, Burn had shrugged and kept a watch for police or security operators. Keeping watch was both useful and helped her ignore the Norwegian metal rappers.

"So, you in or what?"

"Karma's got her H&K," Burn replied, "This should be an easy job, right?"

"I'll double your rate for the trip."

"That's why I grabbed my AK. Triple it."

"Everyone's so distrustful," Micky said, "So mercenary."

"First, we are mercenaries. Second, if you offer to pay more, this is not an easy job."

"So, you're in?"

"Yeah. We have to finish something first. Give us a file on the job. We should be able to pick up in an hour or so."

"Great. You'll have the file in a couple of minutes. I'm out."

"Later."

After a brief pause to lower the volume of the hyper violent song, Burn spoke out loud, "We got the gig with Micky. Looks like we're going to Pittsburgh."

"We'll see all the nicest attractions," Karma said, "And shoot them up."

Chapter 7

"Where's she at?" Hitcher muttered, turning his head to avoid eye contact with the big guy scanning the crowd. A handful of others, more normal sized, were also checking faces. Their hands kept drifting their weapons.

Catching the big guy focusing on him from the corner of his eye, Hitcher shifted to avoid his stare. The man moved toward Hitcher, plowing through the crowd like they were children.

"Son of a bitch," Hitcher said, shifting again, just in case.

With five meters between them, Hitcher found himself brought up short when a woman's hand reached up to his neck. He looked down to see auburn hair stylishly shaved on the sides and long down to her shoulders. A very form fitting suit on a body that worked hard to look that good. His message indicator popped up.

"*I'm your ride out.*"

"There you are, baby. Sorry I took so long. Maria just called and can't make it. You ready?"

"Yeah, sweetie," Hitcher nodded, "Nothing happening here, anyway."

"Something happening at our place real soon."

Glancing over, Hitcher saw the big guy had stopped, confusion evident from his squinting eyes and slight frown. Hitcher walked with the woman to the sports car sitting at the curb, wrapping his arm around her shoulders. The big guy gave him a case of ugly looks but kept his distance. The others, keying off the big guy, froze in their tracks, unsure what to do.

He held the driver's side door open while she got in. The door pulled closed with the efficiency achieved only with expensive engineering. Walking to the other side, he slid into the passenger seat. It killed any machismo he might have had with the locals, but the car and the girl still made him memorable.

She sped through the streets, barely missing the crowds. He smiled and tried to not look like he was checking for anyone following them. Once the car hit the edge of the neighborhood, she gave him a smile that redirected his blood flow away from his brain.

"Two things, big guy," she said, her voice furthering the effect on his blood flow.

"First, the owner of this car is a dick and I'm planning to return it in the same condition it's in now. I want him very surprised when your big friend fucks it completely up."

Hitcher's blood flow reversed course.

"Second, I have a tramp stamp. It happens to be a Ranger tab and my class number. If you try anything I will happily use your body to demonstrate that I also served as a hand to hand combat instructor. This would disappoint Micky. He would probably reduce what he's paying me. Probably."

"I'm going to sit, very quietly, in the passenger seat, miss," Hitcher said, eyes staring straight as the car rocketed down the on ramp to Interstate 75.

"That's a very good idea, my friend," she said, "I've got a great place for us to hang until your ride makes pick up. Now, pass over the data cube you have, and I'll pass you a paycheck."

"It's 3:30," Burn muttered.

"Going on twenty hours so far. We can switch out on the drive, get some rest," Karma said as she guided the sports utility vehicle through the light interstate traffic.

"Yeah. Micky says this might be a little hot. Too hot, and I've got some wake ups that should help out for another twenty hours or so."

"Not saying I hate those things," Karma said, "But they make me edgy."

"Hon, you're edgy after three hours sleep. But, yeah, you have started unnecessary fights on wake ups."

"I don't start unnecessary fights."

"That redneck. The one who's head made the dent in the door at the Dirty Derby," Burn said.

"He kept staring at your tits. He needed a lesson in manners."

"You paid for his medical treatment and signed the bill 'the other chick with great tits.' Really, you could have just slapped him and been done with it."

"People whine when I slap them. Punches and doors get my point across."

"You dented the door at an Atlanta landmark bar. The place was open last century."

"The door was already dented. The owner admits to buying cheap furniture because it gets destroyed so often. I was adding to the decor."

"I don't know how I thought my life was

complete before you came along," Burn said, "Real. Mean it."

"Yeah," Karma turned her eyes on the road, "Don't know what I'd do without ya."

"You'd do fine with or without me, babe. You ready to do the pick up?"

"Pretty much. Get this started, we might get some sleep before next week," Karma said.

"Sending the address. The pay chip cleared, too."

"Got it. Be there in fifteen. We got enough ammo?"

"I went with the variable P."

"P?"

"'P' equals Plenty when doing tactical operations math. Always assume more ammo is better."

"This is one of the reasons we're good together,"

"My sarcastic approach to committing crimes?"

"That and your muffins. I really like your muffins."

"Note to self. Pick up baking supplies when we get back."

"And coffee," Karma said.

"Always coffee."

"A running trail?" Hitcher asked. He had waited an hour before speaking.

"Great place to do hand offs," Sarra said, not looking up from her smart phone.

"It's in the open, anyone can get in here, and there's nowhere to hide."

"The only people who come here are runners and cyclists. They don't care what anyone's doing, as long as they aren't bothering runners and cyclists. There are also frequent police patrols, which means very few people start trouble when the cops will drop on all parties like a C-5 missing three engines."

"I saw that happen once," Hitcher said.

"Cops dropping heavy?"

"No, a C-5 with three dead engines. Up in Cleveland after it went to shit. Everyone was surprised any of them were still flying."

"Third Batt?" Sarra asked.

"Yeah, Alpha Company."

"I was in battalion. That bird hit our base camp."

"We headed in to do recovery. That was a mess. First time we and the Northies ever called a cease fire, since it was their bird."

"Airborne unit that was supposed to jump. Intel confirmed they were hit by friendly fire from a Northie attack helicopter. That's where Colonel Chavez got paid out. XO handled everything well, though."

"You get hurt?"

"Ended up with a broken arm from debris. Got lucky there."

"Didn't get lucky somewhere else?"

"Later in Cleveland. Battalion was operating as a maneuver company, and a Northie managed to hit me with a truck. Literally. A pickup he'd grabbed from who knows where. Broke eight ribs, my back in three places, and both legs."

"Damn."

"Still better than catching a sniper round. Eighty

percent of our dead were from the sniper war going on between our guys and theirs. Your pick up will be here in five minutes."

"So that's why you're able to sit here reading a book in a stolen car and not be stressed."

"Actually, I'm checking the feeds from the video cameras throughout the area," Sarra said, "I'm neither stupid nor trusting, my friend. So, how did you make it through Cleveland?"

"First time, dumb luck and a good squad leader named Micky. Second time? Two bronze stars with V's and five separate purple hearts. Managed to keep my squad up. Barely. Lost four guys in the two months we were in Cleveland the second time."

"Were you trying for the record?"

"No. Way. Sanchez was our first sergeant by then, and he could keep that. Nine hearts in three weeks? Fuck no."

"Two minutes ETA. Good work. Micky was in battalion working the intel shop by then. Mostly, he was going out with a squad of grunts, hacking whatever networks he could, and doing counter sniper ops. Guy was shockingly brilliant at those missions."

"Hell of a Ranger," Hitcher agreed, "One of the few guys I trust implicitly."

"Big word. Remember, Micky always has something he wants, and he never gives anything away for free. He's a patriot, though."

"Those are the reasons I trust him," Hitcher said, "I know he'll use me up to get a job done. I expect that. But he'll tell me up front that he doesn't expect me to make it and to do what I can."

"Smart," Sarra said, "A vehicle will pull up on your side. On my mark, get out and get into the back seat. That's your ride out. Do not ask me questions about them. ETA thirty seconds."

"What're you going to do?"

"Drop this car at its owner's home and make sure video of its location gets to the people hunting you. Because that guy's a real prick and he deserves to have his antique Italian sports car completely trashed by mercs."

"What did he do to you?"

"Forgot to mention that he was married."

Headlights lit the parking space next to them. The SUV was an expensive brand popular with higher income families as a grocery getter.

"Get out."

"Later-"

"Go. Now."

Hitcher got out, took a step, and opened the door to the SUV. He slid into the back seat. Checking the occupants, he found a brunette in the passenger seat, and a blond with blue and red streaks behind the steering wheel.

"Seat belt," the driver said, "Not leaving until you put it on."

"Seriously?" Hitcher asked. He reached over and pulled the seat belt down and across, settling it into the anchor point.

"She never kids about that kind of thing," the passenger said, "I see you're traveling light."

Behind them, the sports car sped into the night.

"She plans to get that beautiful car destroyed," Hitcher said.

"Not our problem," the driver replied, "Just be cool, and we're gone."

"But it's an antique!"

"How much you willing to pay us to stop her?" the driver asked.

"It's not my car," Hitcher said.

"Not our problem, then," the driver said.

"Here's the deal. We're getting you to Pittsburgh. You need to sit quietly, do what we tell you, and we'll get you there without whoever's looking for you actually getting you. Any questions?" the passenger said.

"Two," Hitcher said, "First, who are you two? Second, how does Micky know this many hot women who are apparently way more bad ass than me?"

"First, I'm Burn, she's Karma," the passenger said, "Second, Micky's living right, you aren't. Now sit back and enjoy what we all hope is a very quiet, boring ride."

Hitcher settled back into the seat.

"Yeah, let's hope."

Chapter 8

Hitcher watched Burn pass a pill to Karma, who washed it down with a swallow of coffee. They were heading up the interstate toward South Carolina. Burn was, apparently, searching the internet for somewhere to grab some food.

"There's a place in Greensboro that serves their burgers on buttered buns," Burn said.

"They open?"

"Yeah, looks like they're open twenty four hours," Burn said.

"Pop me the address."

"Oh, wow. They use custard instead of ice cream for their shakes."

"What the fuck?" Karma said, "Don't play around, Burn. I take my shakes seriously."

"Not kidding. Okay, we're on a job. Don't get the shake. We'll try those later. Can't be fuckin' with the mojo when we're earning our paycheck."

"Damn it. See if they serve coffee. I'm out."

"Coffee's a check," Burn said, "So, food stop?"

"When's the last time you ate, hot shot?" Karma asked.

"Eight or nine hours ago," Hitcher said, "Are you two always like this?"

"Sorry, we've been working for about ten hours, and up for twenty or so," Burn said, "Plus, the wake ups make us hungry and edgy."

"Got it," Hitcher said, "Yeah, I could use some food. You guys want me to take a shift on the wheel?"

"No," the women said in unison.

"Better if we drive," Karma said, "Fifteen 'til the food stop."

"You sound like you don't trust me," Hitcher said.

"Listen, we're really good at this kind of thing," Burn said, "We're going to get you across the border, just like Micky wants. It's not about trusting you. We don't. At all. Frankly, I suspect you're an idiot. So, no, we won't be letting you drive. Now sit still and don't make me shoot you."

"I'll stay back here. Any chance of a bacon cheeseburger and a cola?"

"It's on the menu," Burn answered.

Hitcher watched the road lights and the handful of fellow travelers on the interstate. The light traffic was a shock after living so long in Atlanta's constant hustle and action. He breathed in. Some of the stress fade as he exhaled. Burn had made a valid point. Whatever else might happen, he had no control of anything beyond himself. It was a good time to eat whatever they found at the stop and get some rest while he let his transporters handle things.

As they pulled into the parking lot they saw people inside the fast food place. Burn had explained that it was a chain out of the Midwest that opened a few shops in the South. Hitcher sat quietly as Burn and Karma discussed the options.

"Drive through or go in?" Karma asked, watching the people.

"Gonna need a bio break sooner or later," Burn

said, "I'd rather not watch Hitcher hanging out the window for that."

"Going in, weapons hot and hidden. One in the can at a time."

"Good plan. Hitcher, what do you want?"

"Bacon cheeseburger and a cola," He replied.

"Alright," Burn said, "Park and let's do this."

Karma parked the SUV and shut it down. They got out and Hitcher found himself in the odd position of having a lady on each side of him. He also had the feeling that the wrong sound would set the ladies into action. When they stepped around the corner to the door, he saw an immediate problem. The girls glanced at one another and reached some unspoken agreement. Burn pulled the door open.

Scanning the room Hitcher counted a dozen of them, all wearing lots of dark clothing. Patches of bright blue showed through. They were a mix of races. Three women, he noted. The employees, particularly the young lady being pulled across the counter by one of the thugs, looked terrified. Considering they were all showing weapons, several in hand, others holstered but with hands on them, Hitcher understood her fear.

"Oh, we got some more fun walking in," one of them said, laughing.

"We're just here for the food," Burn said, "Let us get our order and it'll be good."

Hitcher wondered, briefly, if Burn was crazy.

"What if we don't want you to leave?" the man asked, a knife dropping into his hand.

Karma stepped forward. Slow pace, easy steps. Just in reach of the guy's knife if he moved. Too close to miss, Hitcher noted. He relaxed. Like it or not, if things went sideways, he was going to act. But it was not his job to call the dance. Breathing out, he waited for Karma and Burn's move.

"Do yourself a favor," Karma said, "Walk out. You play with knives, you'll get hurt."

"I haven't hurt myself yet, little girl," he snapped back.

"I didn't say it would be you causing the hurt," Karma said.

"That a threat, bitch?"

Hitcher was amazed by Karma's speed. It had the feel of implants combined with long experience and practice. She stepped into the man's knife side, grabbed his hand and twisted. His elbow rotated in, forcing his body over, while her free hand plucked the knife from his fingers. The popping sound his wrist made snapping echoed in the room. His head slammed the wall as Karma shifted around to face him. The knife plunged into his shoulder, through the clothes, and embedded in the wall behind him. Blood spread across the man's clothes as he hung there. It had taken less than a second. Hitcher barely had time to curse when everyone moved.

Burn blazed out a magazine worth of ammunition, putting shots into the thugs on the left. Hitcher got his pistol out, barrel toward the ceiling as he crossed behind Karma. The blond left the knife artist stuck to the wall, shrieking, and waded in, the heavy pistol bucking as she went. As he moved, Hitcher casually backhanded the knife guy, his pistol filled hand cutting the shrieks off. The guy slumped, blood dripping from his face to the floor while he hung from the wall.

"Clear!" Burn called out, covering her section of the fight with her pistol.

"Clear!" Karma agreed.

"Not clear," Hitcher stated, walking to the thug who was still reaching across the counter, his hand on the back of the girl's neck. "Let go of her."

"And you'll kill me? Fuck that," the thug spat.

Hitcher very calmly lowered his pistol, his eyes never leaving the thug's. The pistol barked once, and the knee nearest Hitcher folded backward. Blood spilled out of the man's pant leg, leaving a pool on the floor. Hitcher waited until the man collapsed to the floor and then shot his remaining knee. That knee slammed into the counter, leaving a streak of blood and bone fragments. After a few seconds, the shock began to fade and the man began to scream. Hitcher moved to the man's head.

"Fucking wannabe tough guy, wannabe rapist, wannabe piece of shit. I've seen people with legs blown off keep fighting. Shut the fuck up."

Hitcher kicked the man's head into the counter. The screaming stopped.

Turning around, he found Burn and Karma holstering their pistols. Three of the thugs were moaning and clutching wounds. One of them, a woman, was trying to drag herself to the door while holding her stomach. She whimpered as blood smeared across the floor behind her.

"Not bad," Burn said, "A little slow."

"Never got better than the baseline reflex upgrade," Hitcher shrugged, glancing at the girl behind the counter, "Are you guys alright?"

She nodded, along with the other two employees.

"Sorry about the damage," Burn said.

"Any chance we can get our order in?" Karma asked.

"Sure," the guy said, "What are you having?"

"Bacon cheeseburgers," Karma said, "Whatever combo that is, we'll take three of 'em. Large."

"No problem," the guy said, "On the house. Try the root beer. It's really good."

"Man, Jack's gonna be pissed if you do that," the girl said.

"He should have let us keep our guns." the guy said. "And if he doesn't like it, you'll get promoted to shift manager. Now let's get these nice folks some burgers."

"What about them?" the second girl asked, waving her hand across the wounded and dead.

"Fuck 'em," the shift manager said, "They can get burgers somewhere else."

"Short form is you guys have trouble. The Mexicans have a picture of Hitcher in connection to that gang thing in Greensboro," Micky said.

All three were sharing a link to Burn's implant phone so they all heard the statement at the same time. Hitcher groaned. Karma sighed.

"Shit. Which gang?"

"Gang? You wiped the gang out." Micky said, "It's the Holy Mexican Empire you need to focus on. Which means all the Mexican gangs, and pretty much every dropped number out for a paycheck."

Burn glanced at Hitcher, "Holy Mexican Empire? Fuck. What did our friend do?"

"A job. Not relevant other than they want to make an example of him."

"Are you changing our job?" Burn asked.

"Not now. I know you guys are tired. Just deliver him. And try to keep his face out of any cameras. They have pictures they're spreading around. They weren't great images, but good enough that I could make him."

"That's going to take more time. Any idea if they've informed their embassies up there?"

"I'm checking, but so far, I've got nothing," Micky said.

"That could go either way," Karma said, focusing on the road, "Any good news?"

"Someone shot up a gang at a restaurant in Greensboro and the cops aren't looking for a certain stolen SUV. Some Hispanics in the merc community completely trashed a thirty year old Ferrari in Druid Hills a couple of hours ago."

"Tell them they're welcome," Burn said.

"Which one?" Micky asked.

"Greensboro," Hitcher said, his tone clear that he was not going answer any further questions on the other subject.

"Figured." Micky said, "I'll burn the Greensboro footage. Can you three avoid any further unnecessary gun fights?"

"Didn't plan that one." Karma said. "The guy pulled a knife on me. Had to do something."

"Eight dead, two crippled for life if they can't

find a sponsor to pay for implants or bio regen, two more so badly hurt they'll need medical attention for at least two months. Admittedly, with their rap sheets, they'll get their medical from the prison system." Micky said. "I'm locking down the place's video system and burning the footage as fast as I can find it. I know some guys who would buy the footage as a training tool, though. And that won't stop the Mexicans from spreading their copies around."

"Just blank out our faces." Burn said with a sigh. "One day we'll be able to get residuals for that kind of footage."

"Planning on starting a training center?" Micky asked.

"No, the Rangers seem to be putting enough loose cannons on the streets."

"Not fair," Hitcher said, "And I count three former Rangers on the streets."

"Unless you want your apartment to suffer the same fate as an antique sports car recently did, I'd suggest never letting her know you said she was a loose cannon," Micky said.

"Point taken," Hitcher said.

"Hate to cut this short," Karma said, "But fuel's getting low."

"Sounds like you have it in hand," Micky said.

"No," Karma answered, "But give us a few minutes, and we'll have a plan."

"Get to it. I've got security systems to hack."

Chapter 9

Most of the gas station's lights were dead, and a trio of old pickups filled the parking spaces at the store front. Karma pulled off the road and pointed the SUV toward an available pump. Burn scanned the area around them while Karma cut the engine off and opened her door. Hitcher stretched as Karma moved to fuel the SUV. Burn headed for the store, scanning the area as she walked across the concrete.

Several men in rough clothes exited the store as Burn neared the door. One of them held out a sheet to her. Watching, Hitcher noticed the bump of what was likely a pistol under the man's shirt. Burn looked over the sheet and shook her head in the negative before handing it back and heading into the store. His gut tightened at the way some of the men stared after Burn.

Ignoring the girls' directive to stay in the SUV, Hitcher slid across the bench and opened the door. Before Karma could speak, he was out, door shut, and heading to the front of the SUV. The men were five meters away.

A couple of the men, the ones not locked on Burn, noticed him. One of them stared for a moment. Then he looked at the printout in his hand. Head shifted up to look at Hitcher. Hitcher felt a familiar thing, like a stone in his gut. Again, the man looked at the sheet, eyes narrowing in disbelief.

"Shit." Karma said from the far side of the SUV.

The guy was heading for Hitcher, drawing his pistol. His friends saw that and went for their weapons. The harsh neon lights glinted from the bared metal. Karma's pistol barked first, dropping the approaching guy. One of them yelled and then chaos reigned.

Burn was paying for the pile of junk food and three cups of coffee when gun shots vibrated the tough convenience store windows. The clerk pushed a button and thick metal barriers dropped from the ceiling. Her cash chip popped out through a small tray.

"Get the fuck out!" the cashier yelled.

"Watch my food," she barked back, heading for the door.

"Crazy bitch! Get out of here! Fucking psychos!"

"Guess you aren't going to watch my food," Burn said, drawing her pistol as she crouched near the door.

She knew the men were hirelings looking for Hitcher when they showed her the poor quality print. Burn had not guessed that Hitcher would get out of the SUV after he had been told to stay in it.

"*Micky,*" She composed the text on her implant comm, "*Drop every camera and comm tower within two kilometers of my location. Now.*"

Keeping low, she looked over the row of snacks and through the window. The guys were spreading out. Several were down. Karma was leaning into the SUV, and Hitcher was on the other side, firing just enough to keep the group from spreading further. She saw pistols among the men, but nothing heavier.

Breathing deep, she checked the link to her pistol and then pushed the door open with her shoulder. The humidity slapped her as she moved out of the air conditioning. Firing a double tap into the nearest bounty hunter, she was satisfied that they did not have body armor. He spat blood out as he crumpled to the concrete. Low end muscle hoping for an easy payday. They were delivering a lot of pistol ammunition to the SUV, but nothing particularly dangerous.

Karma came out from behind the SUV with her sub machine gun and took a position to Hitcher's right. The blond's lips were pursed, her face emotionless. It was her expression whenever she focused. Burn shot two more of the group, double tapping each man from the side. A couple of them noticed their friends falling, taking their attention away from Karma.

Three bursts from the sub machine gun took down three of the men. Hitcher caught another one with a bullet to the shoulder. Given the range, Burn decided not to waste rounds shooting double taps. She lined up the red dot from the gun link on a head and pulled the trigger. Brains and bone sprayed across the others. A heartbeat later, she fired again. The bounty team's numbers were dropping fast. Another burst from Karma cut their numbers again. Blood began to flow toward the rain grates in the concrete.

Some sense of tactics must have penetrated the surviving four's brains. With limited options, they turned toward Burn. Burn fired twice more, switching back to double tapping them. Two fell, ravaged by the heavy caliber bullets. One turned and ran toward Karma and Hitcher, falling to their fire. The last had an evil grin as the pin dropped to the ground. His arm was in motion but cut short by a combination of Burn and Karma shooting him simultaneously.

The impacts caused his body to twitch. His grenade arched high, bounced as the safety spoon popped away, and rolled under the SUV. His body collapsed as the grenade rolled. Burn shot him again, on principle, and backed away. Karma was already moving, shoving Hitcher ahead of her, toward the corner of the store. Burn sprinted toward the store's industrial safety glass doors.

She found herself rolling from the concussion of the fragmentation grenade's detonation. Her back slammed into the doors, forcing them inward. Covering her face, she tried to tuck and roll with the shock wave. Stinging bits of white hot metal peppered her hands, the smell of burned skin spreading as she crashed to the ground. Air ripped out of her body from the impact, leaving her gasping as she tried to orient herself.

"What the fucking hell?" came from the still contained cashier's box.

"Grenade," Burn answered, "That hurt."

"Is that you, crazy bitch?"

"Yes, it is, asshole."

"How did you survive that?"

"Body armor," Burn answered, "I think it was an old frag. Probably something his daddy or granddaddy brought back from Afghanistan."

"Grenades? Afghanistan? They didn't look like terrorists."

"Probably weren't," Burn said, sitting up, "Probably low rent bounty hunters."

"Why were they trying to kill you?"

"Mistaken identity," Burn said.

"Mistaken?"

"Yeah. They mistook us for people who wouldn't fight back," Burn said, "I'm gonna need more coffee."

"This was supposed to be 'easy job'," he complained.

"Cry me a river, asshole," Burn replied, "So is mine."

"This is real simple," Karma told Hitcher, who stretched across the narrow back seat of the pickup. Flames still licked out from under the SUV and jetted from the wrecked gas pump next to it. The broken line was burning a jet of gas. Burn handed out cups of coffee.

"If Burn or I tell you to stay in the truck. Stay. In. The. Fucking. Truck."

"Yeah, got it," Hitcher said.

"If you don't, I'll shoot you until you can't get out of the truck. Push too much, I'll deliver you to the Mexicans myself and send Micky video of the delivery. Got it?"

"Got it. Really, got it. I fucked up. I didn't mean to get us into a gun fight. I can't fix what I did, and I can't bring those poor bastards back. I won't fuck up again. Swear it."

"I have a question." Burn said, "Were you

shooting to wound, Hitcher?"

"Yeah, I guess I was."

"You new to this?"

"Kinda."

"So, let me get his straight," Burn said, "Tonight was your first job, wasn't it?"

"I've got a back-"

"First job," Karma cut him off.

"So, first job was tonight, and you went into the Mexican embassy solo, made it out, and have been in two gun fights since then."

"Nice summary," Hitcher said, facing the window.

Driving out of the convenience store parking lot, Karma finally spoke, "Not bad. For a newb."

"Seen worse," Burn said in agreement.

"Not kidding about shooting you, though. We got a long way to go, and less attention is better."

"I thought I'd covered that. Stay in the truck. Don't move unless I'm told to. Follow instructions. Got it."

"Good."

"Would you feel bad about shooting me?" Hitcher asked after a moment.

"No, she won't," Burn said.

"Okay, that's fair. One more question."

"Depends on the question," Burn said.

"How did you two get so damn good? Even most Rangers weren't that calm under fire. Not even Micky."

"I got some good training," Burn said.

"I was born this way," Karma said.

"I have comms. Keep your comm shut down,

Hitcher. No sense taking chances. They definitely have your description. I'll update Micky and see what he can do for us."

Her eyes glazed over, but that did not stop Burn from turning in her seat and conducting a rapid and professional pat down of Hitcher.

"What the hell?" He sat up as she ran her hands over his body.

"No injuries. Eyes on the road, Karma."

"I'm cool," the blond answered.

Burn ran her hands over her partner. Hitcher could swear that she added an extra squeeze on the blond's thigh. If she had, the blond did not acknowledge. Clearly the women were more than just business partners, but the blond's aloofness seemed to extend even to Burn. Whatever their issue was, it was one Hitcher chose to leave alone. It was not his business, and he had done enough to anger them for the trip. A wave of weariness washed over him.

Chapter 10

"Where are we?" Hitcher rubbed his eyes as the sun blinded him.

"Kentucky," Karma said, "Changed route plans again."

"Why?"

"We're blown. Cops are not happy about gun fights in interstate convenience stores, and Micky couldn't squash all the video that had rolled out before he cut the cameras. So, we've got the cops, the Mexicans, and mercs looking for a pay day after us. Changing routes seemed like a good idea."

"Yeah, sounds like the only option."

"Radio silent, by the way," Karma said, "We turned off your comms, and they'll stay down until we have you in place and Micky confirms you're where he wants you. Micky did the shutdown. Check the rest of your 'plants. They should be signaling direct rather than trying to use the wireless feeds."

Hitcher set off the diagnostics program for his implants. After a few seconds, he received up signals, other than his communications implant. It was hard down.

"Yeah, I'm good," Hitcher said, "How long have you been awake?"

"Thirty hours, give or take," Karma said, "No, you can't drive. I'm fine."

"How many wake ups have you taken?"

"About sixty percent fewer than your low end guess," Karma said, "Mostly coffee right now. We should get some sleep cycles tonight."

"Not going to tell me the plan, are you?"

"Not a chance. Can't spill or screw up what you don't know," Karma said, "This gig, Burn's the lead, I'm the trigger puller. Her plan, and I don't ask. Can't tell what I don't know."

"Big on compartmentalization. So, can I ask where you got your implants."

"Born with 'em."

"Unlikely."

"If you ever get back to Atlanta, Doc Stone over in the Techwood free clinic does some nice work on the side." Karma shrugged, "Good materials. Knows his business."

"I'll keep that in mind. You haven't asked me."

"Not going to, either. Not my business."

"All business, are you?"

"That's how it is."

"Interesting way to work," Hitcher said, "At least she doesn't snore."

Karma let the comment pass, eyes scanning the road, the controls, and the rear-view mirrors.

"So, everyone's looking for us, and we're in a stolen ride last seen at a location we shot a bunch of guys."

"Pretty much," Karma said.

"I don't think this plan is such a great idea," Hitcher said.

"Why's that? Since you don't actually know the plan."

"Because the cops are probably looking for this truck?" Hitcher said.

"You have so little faith," Karma said, "A valid point, but little faith."

"Give me a reason to trust."

"I haven't shot you."

"You're getting paid not to."

"Alright, bright boy. We're in a pickup, the second most common personal vehicle in the northern portion of the Southern States. It happens to be red, which is the most common color of pickup. There are no bullet holes in it, so anyone looking for it is looking for a lot of different vehicles. And, even if Micky didn't get the initial video, he got a lot of it, and he's blocking searches for us. So, there are a few things in our favor."

"Would a car full of people with guns be one of those things in our favor?" Hitcher said.

"Probably not. Why?"

"Because there's one behind us about to pass, and they're giving us the hairy eyeball."

"Shit." Karma said, "Just be cool."

"Does being cool include pulling my pistol out?"

"As long as they don't see it, I'm good with that."

"Then I'm ice. We going to wake Burn up?'

"Not yet. They might just be heading to the border."

"Passing," Hitcher said.

"Watching them."

"Fuck's going on?" Burn slurred the words as her eyes opened.

"Possible problems." Karma said, "Go back to sleep."

"Problem?"

"I got it."

"'Kay," Burn leaned her head against the door.

"Keep your head down, Hitcher," Karma said,

"Just be cool."

"They got friends coming up." Hitcher said after he shifted in the back seat. "This is fucked."

"Making a note to find out what's going on. After we get through this."

"Good idea." Hitcher said, "Might want to wake Burn up."

"She's awake." Karma said, "She just wishes she wasn't."

"Both true statements. Got numbers?"

"Three cars. Two behind, one ahead, and slowing down for us to catch up. I think they want to keep us on the highway."

"Options?"

"Go off road with this thing. Not sure how it'll handle. Wait for the attack, and react. We aren't in a good position to deal with a rolling defensive fight. Last, go on offense, take the lead car, and then try to get clear."

"We'll get shot up from behind," Burn said.

"I'm big, slow and been shot a lot of times before this," Hitcher said.

"Not funny."

"Is funny," Karma said, "But not what we're getting paid for. Give him your rifle, he keeps the shitheads off of us once it gets going."

"Hitcher, lay down like you're going to take a nap," Burn said, "My rifle's under the seat. Karma, I've got yours. You focus on driving. Get us out of this box before they close the sides up."

"We've got ten seconds before we catch up with the lead car. Heavy car, too. Ramming is not an option."

"Ramming would destroy our engine." Burn said, "Just say 'go' when we're close enough to shoot them."

Burn rested her finger on the window's switch and waited, trying to look like she was still waking up. Karma was focused on driving and tracking the vehicles that were drawing closer. Hitcher waited for the signal, planning to open the rear split windows and do what he could. Taking a long breath, he wondered if this was going to work.

"Go!" Karma yelled, "Coming up fast!"

Hitcher jerked the split window open. A second later, he noted the link to the rifle's sighting system had synced with the induction pad in his palm. One of the trail cars was moving to the passing position, and the passengers were readying weapons. Hitcher felt the trigger, took up slack and waited for the targeting dot to settle on the driver. He pulled the trigger and felt the burst of rounds hammer the rifle into his shoulder. The window spider-webbed, with a single hole punched through it. Before he could reset the sights, the car veered to the left, off the shoulder, and into the ditch. Unlike all the action shows he had watched as a kid, the car rolled twice but did not blow up. It settled on the crushed roof, wheels spinning in the air. An arm stuck out of one window.

Shooters in the second car fired back, hitting high or into the tailgate of the truck. Their weapons were light, so the rounds did not punch through. The scant protection failed at making Hitcher feel better. He ducked down and tried to get a sight on the driver. The car weaved back and forth. The evasive maneuver caused the car to fall back.

"This seriously sucks. Why didn't those assholes have some armor on this thing?" Hitcher said.

"Because they were expecting to follow their target and not get shot at by maintaining good distance?" Karma asked, "Burn, I'm gonna close on the lead car. See if you can do something about them."

"Go." Burn grinned, "I'll light them up."

Karma shoved the gas pedal to the floor boards. The truck had a strong engine meant for pulling and towing. With no weight to hold it back the truck surged forward. Hitcher settled himself in the rear window again, sighted in, and let off a burst toward the trail car. He missed, but the car backed off.

Checking over his shoulder showed him Burn shooting a burst into the lead car. The rear window spider-webbed. Burn adjusted the sub machine gun and fired again. One of the car's occupants flopped out the passenger window as the rounds chewed through his armor. He slipped out, hitting the asphalt head first. The corpse rolled off the road, leaving a smear of brains and blood.

"One down." Burn called out, "Live one in the middle, though."

"Shoot him," Karma suggested over the wind.

Burn drove herself out the window. The lead car shifted to the empty oncoming lane, forcing her to lean out and shift onto the pickup's hood. A machete cleared out the car's rear window, and a huge man shoved himself out. Hitcher checked on the trail car. It was closing again. Two bursts backed it off, one of them plugging the car's radiator. Steam billowed from under the car's hood.

Glancing forward, he turned just in time to see Burn fire on the lead car again, stitching the trunk. The guy with the knife glared at her, chrome eyes focused on Burn. He stuck his knife into the trunk and pulled himself forward.

"Watch the rear!" Karma said.

Hitcher swung back and ducked under the rounds hitting the cab. Biting off a curse, he shifted until the caret was centered on the rear quarter of the hood, and fired a long burst. The car spun to the right, the passenger side front tire blowing out from the pressure of the fast turn. The rim caught in the soft shoulder, and the car flipped. It rolled over into the ditch and slammed to a stop. No one came out of the vehicle.

"Rear is clear," Hitcher said.

"Great." Karma said, "Help out up front."

Turning, Hitcher was surprised to find the knife guy trying to get stable enough to jump to the truck. Burn had put some rounds on him, but nothing serious. Not for lack of trying. His armor was chewed up, the steel plates under showing the impacts.

"Going out your window," Hitcher said.

"No, grab the wheel," Karma said.

"What?"

"Wheel! Now!"

Hitcher leaned over the front seat, taking the steering wheel in hand while he shoved the Kalashnikov out of the way. Karma kept a steady foot on the gas while she pulled her pistol out. Shifting it to her left hand, she reached across and hit the window down button. Burn kept the knife man pinned with pot shots. With all the action, Hitcher was having trouble keeping the truck going straight. He settled for keeping it on the road.

Karma waited for Burn's burst. The blond popped out the window, her foot pressing the gas pedal down as Burn scrambled back in. Burn dropped the empty magazine from the sub machine gun, grabbed another one from the bag on the floor board and fought her way back out. Hitcher glanced over to see Karma taking steady shots at the lead car. With his twitching of the wheel it was a guess as to whether she was shooting for the car or the knife guy.

Burn yelled something to Karma as she used the hood for a shooting rest and fired a stream of rounds into the car's trunk. Karma waved her hand to the left, so Hitcher eased the wheel left. The knife guy shifted his head from one girl to the other. His scowl in suspicion. When he looked back to Burn, Karma shoved the gas pedal to the floor.

Hitcher made a mental note to congratulate Karma for surprising the knife guy. His head snapped up, focusing on the truck grill rushing at him. He tensed his legs, preparing to leap. Karma shot three times, each round spaced enough that Hitcher was sure she was aiming. He could not tell what she was aiming for until the car jerked left. The blond shifted her weight again, holding the gas pedal down. Hitcher grabbed Burn's belt while he pulled the wheel to the right.

Shock jerked his arm. The truck hammered into the car's rear, adding energy to its spin. Looking out, he saw the knife guy bounce off the driver's door of the truck and miss getting a hold on the side mirror. Karma slid in, shooting at the guy while her free hand grabbed the wheel. Burn tumbled back into the truck.

"Eyes on the road, Karma," Burn called, "Hitcher, cap that asshole."

Hitcher twisted around, working the rifle out the window. His target was rolling down the highway, while the car he had been on rolled over going corner to opposite corner. Settling the caret on the guy as best he could, he squeezed out a burst. Missed completely. Taking a deep breath, he settled into the stock, waited for the sight to land, and fired again.

His target took the shots as he stood up. Hitcher switched his vision to maximum magnification. Knife boy was battered, beat up, and bleeding, but he was standing and glaring at the truck.

"One tough mother fucker," Hitcher said as the target drifted out of the rifle's range, "Rolled off that, and I hit him at least once."

"I'd bet we'll see him again," Burn said.

"I hope," Karma said.

"You plan to fuck him or fight him?" Burn asked.

"Yes," Karma white knuckled the wheel.

Chapter 11

"Been a long time since I was in Cincinnati," Hitcher muttered.

They hiked along a country road heading toward Cincinnati. Sweat ran down Hitcher's back. He glanced at the clouds building up above them. Neither of his escorts had mentioned weather. Nothing about their bearing indicated any change would be made if the weather turned.

"Business?" Burn asked.

"Rangers. Cincinnati was pretty early for me. Micky was my squad leader then. Compared to Cleveland, Cincinnati was easy days."

"Anyone going to recognize you?" Burn asked.

"Pretty sure I shot anyone who was already mad. Everyone else was just trying to find a place to stay safe while the troops had it out."

"Best news I've heard all day." Burn said, "I hate hiking."

"Good news, then," Karma said, "We can camp in the timber ahead, wait until dark and go in. If we stick to the wrecked areas, probably won't have any problems that we can't solve with violence."

"Violence is the last resort of the incompetent," Hitcher said with a chuckle.

"Violence is the first resort of the capable." Karma replied, "And, yes, violence solves problems. Dead people aren't known for getting revenge."

"It was a joke." Hitcher said, "Looks like it might rain."

"Then we'll be wet."

"Touchy much?" Hitcher said.

"She's not being touchy. Karma gets really focused when we're working. Comes off as abrasive most of the time."

"You put up with it?"

"It's how she's wired." Burn shrugged, "It's not like she's always like this, just when we're working. Between the wake ups and the lack of sleep, she should either be way more bitchy or falling down by now."

"So what's keeping you two moving today?"

"Job to do." Burn said, "We'll get a few hours up here, find a ride tonight or in the morning, get some food, and get you dropped off."

"Is it that simple?"

"Probably not." Burn said, "I'm surprised we haven't run into more bounty hunters and mercs. I was expecting some kind of action at the border."

"It's going too smoothly, so there's a shit storm coming?" Hitcher asked.

"Some times. Nothing we did and bad luck the Mexicans got a picture of you. Micky called us for a reason. That reason is we do the job. So, we'll deliver you and get our pay. With a little luck, we've left the trouble behind us."

"We're carrying an arsenal in a nation that barely allows it's cops to carry guns," Hitcher said.

"I have no explanation for why the cops don't leave." Burn said with a shrug, "Bad upbringing, I suppose."

"Or it's home, so they stay and do the job." Hitcher said, "When the fighting wrapped up, there were a lot of meetings between our units and their units. Everyone had forgotten that we were all one country a few years ago. All those soldiers were just people doing what they felt was right and patriotic. Those same feelings were why the battles grew so terrible. Cleveland One was a meat grinder. Cleveland Two? The military historians on all sides say Cleveland Two was likely to exceed the total body counts of every previous urban battle. We completely smoked the total casualties in Stalingrad in less than a month."

"So, what's the plan for transportation?" Karma interrupted.

"Depends." Burn said, "If we can buy something, I'm good with that. Otherwise, we'll try to steal something that won't be noticed for a few hours."

"Doing a lot of grand theft auto," Karma said, "Combined with the guns, we're looking at a long term prison stretch if we get caught."

"Walking to Pittsburgh would suck." Burn said, "Worth the risk to get wheels."

"Cincinnati has a pretty deep criminal network." Karma said, "Maybe get in with them, make a fast buy, and go."

"That'll let people know someone's in town." Burn said, "Might be better to do it ourselves. Cops looking for a stolen car will look local first."

"Get one right after the owner gets home, and we've got odds of it not being called in until morning," Karma said.

"Works." Burn said, "Let's find a camp and get some sleep."

"Rain coming," Hitcher said.

"Like I said," Karma said, "We'll live with

getting wet."

"She's good," Hitcher said.

"Yes, she is." Karma answered, "Now keep quiet."

Hitcher shifted through visual spectrums until he spotted Burn's outline in a faint green glow. Burn crouched next to the sedan. He let out the breath he was holding as she approached the car without a car alarm going off. The neighborhood was full of small houses and drive ways, but it was solid enough that Hitcher expected a quick response from law enforcement. From his conversations with his escorts, he wanted nothing to do with cops.

Moving cautiously, Burn produced something from inside her jacket and quickly had the car door open. While she was slipping into the driver's seat, Hitcher shifted his gaze to the house. There were lights on, but no one was near the windows. He took a long, slow breath to keep from holding it. So far, it looked like they were having a spell of good luck.

The car started. He barely heard it from across the street. A gentle pull at his jacket reminded him that Karma was there. With a turn of her head, she directed him toward the end of the alley where they would link up with Burn. He crouched until Burn backed the car out of the driveway.

Jogging up the alley, Hitcher scanned the road and tried to be silent. Arousing the ire of some family dog would draw attention. No one ignored a barking dog at eleven in the evening, particularly on a week night. Other than a cat hissing at them, they reached the end of the alley unnoticed, where the sedan waited.

Karma slid into the passenger seat, leaving Hitcher to shrug his tall body into the back seat. After a moment of twisting around, he put his feet into the floor board of the passenger side and stretched along the back bench seat.

"You good back there?" Burn asked.

"Good as I'll get." Hitcher replied, "Next time, I'll just fly out of Hartsfield."

"You flown lately? Seats are horrible." Burn said, "I have no leg room. You'll end up choking some idiot for setting his seat back."

"Thanks for the tip," Hitcher grumbled as Burn drove.

Hitcher spent the next fifteen minutes checking every angle. He knew that a local or a cop who regularly patrolled the area would recognize the car. Once recognized, they would want to know what the driver was doing out later than normal. Knowing that once spotted they were going to have trouble, he hoped to spot trouble before trouble spotted them.

"Relax." Karma said, "Even if they see the car, they can't see us. Light changes, tinted windows, all that plays to our favor. Most people, if they recognize the ride, will figure the owner had to run out for something."

"Yeah, sorry. Little nervous."

"We're currently looking at five to ten in Joliet," Burn said, "You could probably cut a deal and give up names and get a shorter stretch or a nicer joint."

"You serious?"

"Keep in mind, sooner or later, we'll get out. And then we'd come find you." Burn said, "But, yeah, you could do that. It's going to be a worse term after we pick up the guns. Fifteen years, minimum, for each gun. At that point, I'd actually recommend you cut a deal."

"I'd prefer not getting caught." Karma said, "If it's all the same."

"Right there with you," Hitcher agreed.

"Then we're back to the 'relax' plan," Burn said, "And, if we have to deal with cops, make it fast, brutal, and out of view of their cameras."

"Cameras?" Hitcher asked.

"Northie cops have to wear cameras that record everything they encounter, do, and say. No choice. Makes dealing with them a pain in the ass. Keeps on duty police abuse of authority and questionable shootings pretty rare, though," Burn said, eyes checking the mirror.

"So, if they catch us, they'll have us on camera?"

"Which means, when operating up here, the first step of every plan is to avoid any and all contact with law enforcement," Karma said.

"That gets just as interesting as you think." Burn said, "And as tricky."

"Oh, shit."

"Yeah. Now, relax. We're gonna get the guns and some pastries and coffee and get you to Pittsburgh."

Chapter 12

Hitcher shifted his feet around the blanket covering the seventy five years worth of guns. Burn and Karma were in an all night coffee shop, getting grub for the road trip. If they were concerned about cops or the Mexicans and their hirelings getting hold of them, Hitcher had not noticed. All things considered, though, if anyone did show up, he was going to grab a gun and hope the girls were close enough to help.

Checking the door to the coffee shop for the tenth time, the women came out. Burn balanced a carrier with four cups, her other hand carrying a sack. Karma juggled three bags in each hand. Seconds later, they were in the car, pushing bags at Hitcher. He moved as fast as he could to place the sacks on the seat.

"Did you leave anything for the next customers?" Hitcher asked.

"We got all the canoli," Karma said, "They were making more, but we decided not to wait."

"Canoli?" Hitcher asked, "Did you get anything that might be healthy?"

"Couple of sandwiches in one of the bags," Burn said, "But the canoli are amazing."

"You two are crazy," Hitcher said.

"Yes, we are." Karma agreed, starting the car, "Coffee, please."

Burn placed a cup in Karma's cup holder and handed another cup back to Hitcher.

"You need cream and sugar?" Burn asked

"Why do I feel like that's the set up for a joke?"

Hitcher said.

"Not if you caught on that fast. Got both in a bag. Not as good as the stuff inside, but it'll do," Burn replied.

"I'll go with black." Hitcher shrugged, "Got used to it that way in the Army and never have gotten into the whole cream and sugar thing."

"Works for me." Burn said with a shrug, "Your second cup's in the other holder, Karma."

"Cool. Seat belt on." Karma said, "Both of you."

"You're worried about seat belts now?"

"Single most common cause for being pulled over in Northern cities is not wearing a seat belt," Karma said, "Since that stop will not end well for us, let's avoid being stopped."

"We spend a lot of time checking out things like that." Burn said, "Beats learning the hard way."

Hitcher pulled the belt around himself. Burn was doing the same, with her coffee in her free hand. She turned toward him once the clasp locked.

"Pass me a canoli," Burn said.

Hitcher unrolled the top of a bag and handed one to her. She managed to work the wrapper off with one hand while Karma pulled onto the street. The scent of the pastry filled the car, blending with the trio's sweat and the coffee. Chewing slowly, Burn finally swallowed and washed it down with a sip of coffee.

"Oh, that's amazing." Burn said, "So very good."

"I'm making a note of the place's name and address." Karma said as she headed toward the interstate, "We might have to make that a regular stop."

"We'll see if they deliver and make sure to get the word out. Another, please."

Hitcher passed a canoli to Burn.

"Pass the word?" Hitcher asked.

"Yeah. Word gets out about the place and no one bothers it. Plus, their business goes up. With a little luck, in a year or so we get a franchise in Atlanta and won't have to set up smuggling runs to get canoli this good."

"Mind if I try one?" Hitcher asked.

"Go ahead." Burn said, "Careful, though. Don't know if there are any places in Pittsburgh with canoli like this."

Chapter 13

"There's no way it's this easy," Karma said, passing a "Welcome to Pittsburgh" sign.

"How many people do you have to shoot for it to be 'just right'?" Hitcher asked.

"She's right. No one's bothered us since the border." Burn said, "We've stopped for gas, slept, and grabbed more food. Took nearly a day to cover five hours of driving. The car has to have been reported stolen. Someone is sitting on those reports."

"Micky?"

"Radio silence. When we stopped contacting him, Micky should have gotten the idea and let us roll. And even Micky would have a tough time wading through false negatives with that many road options to work through. Won't write it off, but unlikely that he would keep putting out waves to find us after the first hour or two."

"Okay, fair," Hitcher said, "But the Mexicans have even less to work with. Where would they even start?"

"Knife dude." Karma said, "He had a good description of the truck, and the road we were on. Fewer options to wade through."

"They find the truck, they have a good idea of where to start looking. Odds are the knife guy had cybereyes, so figure he's got camera footage and a good look at Karma and I, at least. Probably you, too. With a good starting, and the money for good hackers and their internal people, it's very possible they got a look at us in Cincinnati. Hell, the northern states are wired for sound, pictures, and body temperatures.

The Mexicans will assume we're going for car theft and focus on tracking down those leads. Which means we had, if they don't have current camera feeds on us, about a day to get you somewhere safe or dropped off with whoever Micky wants you packed up with."

"How're you going to figure that out?"

"Throw away phones," Karma said.

"Get 'em in every convenience and big box store on the continent." Burn shrugged, "Unlike good canoli. Still, we get one here, one there, call Micky and get instructions. Move on. Use the next phone. I'm betting the Mexicans are closing in on us, but I figure we have at least four hours, maybe six, before they can get a good track on us."

"What happens when they do?"

"Kill 'em. Move to the next point. Micky has to have someone in the area that can get you to ground. Once you're with them," Karma said, "Either we can finish the Mexicans' hirelings, or we get out."

"So, you two can handle all the mercs by yourselves?"

"If they have images of us, odds are they've found some rumors about us." Burn said, "Might back them off, if we can get you dropped off first."

"If not? Or if they decide to make an example of you?" Hitcher asked.

"Oh, that's easy." Karma said, "We hammer them."

"Again, they probably won't make it that simple."

"They've got limits." Karma said, "We're backed in the corner. There's no reason to not make a big mess. From the looks of things, Pittsburgh might appreciate having a shitty neighborhood leveled."

"This isn't Cleveland." Burn said, "And Detroit, at least the areas farthest from ground zero, are doing better now. Granted, they have a lot less population strain."

"Hmm." Hitcher said, "Might be interesting to stay around for that."

"Trust me, if Karma intends to go all urban renewal, you do not want to be there." Burn shook her head, "It is not happy making."

"You make it sound like she would have been good in the Rangers." Hitcher said, raising an eyebrow.

"Possibly. Based on her skill set, I'd go with the Seminole Winds." Burn said, "She's never mentioned. Kind of impolite to ask, you know."

"Yeah." Hitcher shrugged, "It does get annoying. So, how about we go buy some phones."

"Good idea," Burn said.

"Where the fuck have you been?" Micky said, struggling to keep his voice reasonable. Shouting at Burn never worked. At best, she would hang up, dump Hitcher in the most hellish place she could find, and not take his calls for a week. If he said just the right thing, though, she would come pay him a visit. He had heard rumors about someone threatening her during a call. The rumor was all it took.

"A little busy. Pretty sure you've got a leak

somewhere. Fuckers were finding us way too fast."

"I got the idea you might be worried about something like that." Micky said, "I've gone on a security revamp since you went quiet."

"Nice. Figured out where we've been?"

"Three cars trashed, lots of bullet holes, and eleven dead." Micky said, "The bluegrass law enforcement community is considering a head bounty on you, if they figure out who you are."

"Should have been twelve. One dude walked away."

"You let him go?"

"No, he jumped off a car, missed our ride, rolled on the highway, and then our passenger shot him," Burn said, "Bald guy, just a bit under two meters, masses about a hundred, hundred and five kilos, chrome eyes, tanned skin, and a damn big knife."

"I'll get a profile on that guy. Has to have a reputation I can track down."

"Go one better. I got a picture for you." Burn said, "And getting it loaded to this piece of shit phone was not easy."

"Okay, send it. Can't hurt." Micky said, "Since I'm assuming this number is going to end up in a sewer somewhere, what's next?"

"We're going to hole up and make contact with you. We'll vector to your contacts here as we go," Burn said.

"Works for me. I'll get arrangements made. Anything else you need from me?"

"Ammo, trigger pullers, and beers." Burn said, "Karma's sure we're going to be seeing knife guy again, and he'll probably have friends."

"Got the pic. Working on that. Get to ground and get in touch when it's safe."

"I'll call when I can."

The call dropped. Micky could imagine Burn breaking the phone and tossing pieces into a storm drain as she walked. She was probably right about a leak, but there was little he could do at the moment. With any luck, the security hacks he had implemented would buy some time. In the time he had, Micky brought up the number of an operator in Pittsburgh who could use and train Hitcher. Hitcher was good, but he needed some refinement to be useful in the spy war that North America had become.

"Yo, Banger, my guy made it. You ready to pick him up?" Micky said as soon as the call was answered.

"That place looks good," Burn said as Karma circled an abandoned factory.

Hitcher looked over the building. Every window was broken, sharp edges reflecting street light. The doors he could see were damaged, several hanging by what bolts had not rusted away. Giving it some thought, he wondered if the building had been hit during the war. Most of the area looked like an urban combat zone that was being reclaimed, a meter at a time, by locals desperate for shelter.

"Yeah," Hitcher said, "It'll do."

"Do for what?" Burn asked.

"If the Mexicans or the knife guy are looking for

me." Hitcher said, "This is a good place for what happens when they come."

"You got a plan?" Karma said.

"Yeah." Hitcher said, "I got a plan."

"Spill," she pulled the car through a turn.

"Make it clear I'm here, let the locals see me. Wait for 'em. Most likely they'll come at night, so there's time to get some things set up. When the sun drops, bait 'em in. Make the bastards earn their pay, if they can collect at all."

"As plans go," Burn said, "that one is lean."

"Not the worst plan we've ever dealt with," Karma said.

"Not a lot to work with," Burn said.

"He's over explaining," Karma said.

"Oh?"

"Shorten it up. We let 'em know we're here, and when they come for us, we send 'em to hell."

"I like it." Burn said, "I can work with that."

"I think you two missed something," Hitcher said.

"What's that?" Burn asked.

"You've done your job. I'm in Pittsburgh. You got no stake in this, and I can't afford to pay you for it."

"Chivalry isn't dead," Burn said with a chuckle.

"Fuck chivalry." Karma said, "Knife boy thinks he's the nasty blade artist. I'm going to take him down and then out."

"Did you miss the part about this not being your fight?" Hitcher said.

"He's all yours, Karma." Burn said, "We can keep his friends busy so you can have knife boy all to yourself."

"You two aren't listening," Hitcher said.

"We heard you." Karma said, "We considered your opinion. Now we're ignoring it. Deal with it. We're in 'til it's over, Hitcher."

"You know that guy has you by thirty centimeters and probably fifty kilos," Hitcher said.

"Hitcher, if she starts grinning, I'm going to punch you. After we deal with the shit storm that's coming."

"Since you two are clearly not doing the smart thing," Hitcher said, "let me ask what makes you so sure that shit storm is coming?"

Burn glanced at Karma. Hitcher checked the rear-view mirror saw the blond grinning.

"You're getting punched. I'm going to have Micky give knife boy a call. Save us some time, and keep us from having to sleep in a junked out factory."

"Burn, this is crazy." Micky said, "Even for you two."

"We settle it now or the Mexicans will be hunting for your boy until they get him. Make it clear that their pride is going to be paid for in a lot of hard to explain bodies across two countries. Even machismo takes second place to smart international politics."

"That wasn't the part I think is crazy." Micky said, "Although I will concede the point on politics. This guy is a one man wrecking crew. He's got a reputation and he's done the killing to make it clear he earned it."

"Then why haven't we heard of him?" Burn's voice came through with heavy sarcasm over the analog disposable cell phone she was using.

"Because you two don't work the Reconquista lands much. He's done a lot to keep the partisans down to a dull roar, when they aren't running scared. The Mexicans brought him in for this because they figured he could get it settled before it become too noticeable."

"Well, we've decided someone needs to send a message to the Mexicans. This guy is the message. He got a name? Or is he just a random nameless bad ass that only they can control?"

"Emiliano Zapata is the name he works under out west." Micky said, "Took it from a revolutionary leader back in the early twentieth century Mexican history. I'd give more, but I just had time to scan a pedia entry after I got the name."

"Great, he knows his history. What else you got on him?"

"He's never met a cybernetic implant he didn't like, and the Mexicans keep him on the bloody razor blade. Likes close in work, especially blades. Good with guns in a fight but not big on sniping. Usually has to have someone else provide long cover. He's at least as heavily modded as you, probably more so. He's been pushing feelers trying to find you three, and he's hiring a fresh crew with Mexican money."

"So he's getting a team?"

"Got no numbers for sure, but it's reading like he's got a short platoon."

"Alright," Burn said, "Gonna need some

supplies for that."

"You sure you want me to vector Zapata in on you?"

"Me? I'm ambivalent other than the message piece," Burn said.

"You're ambivalent about fighting him?"

"I never said I was going to fight him. And Hitcher does have some skills, but he's not fighting Z-man, either. Karma, however, is all over that shit." Burn said, "She's going to make sure the message that goes back is 'We'll send your absolute best back in body bags, and they will definitely need a closed casket.'"

"You didn't tell me it was Karma gunning for him."

"On the subject of Karma, did you ever find anything connecting her to the Winds?"

"Nah, nothing." Micky said, "Although they would like to recruit her if she's interested. You, too, for that matter. Something about your reputation, they figure you'll fit right in."

"I doubt I'm Seminole." Burn said, "And I don't think Karma is."

"The Seminole sometimes accepted people who survived the swamps into the tribe. You two have a reputation for surviving dangerous places, so I guess they'd extend the courtesy."

"I'll let Karma know." Burn said, "Maybe after our trip, we'll give them a call. So, can you get us some gear and get that metaled up whack job headed to us?"

"I'll see what I can do about gear. May not be much in the area." Micky said, "After that, I'll let him know he's got a fan club that would love a one on one."

"Perfect. Now off you go to have some artillery misallocated to us."

"Gone and doing," Micky cut the call.

Chapter 14

The truck ground over debris as it pulled away, leaving pelican cases of gear behind. Burn watched as Karma wiped sweat from her brow and pushed a lock of hair behind her ear. Hitcher was checking the tension on a tripwire. Taking a deep breath, Burn offered her water bottle to Karma.

"Thanks," Karma said.

"You're cute when you're sweaty," Burn said.

"You're always cute," Karma said, "Except when you're beautiful."

"This is a bad time for me to walk up?" Hitcher said.

"Depends on why you were walking," Burn said.

"I'll go with getting a time frame for the attack," Hitcher said.

Burn and Karma exchanged looks. Karma shrugged and walked toward the central office. Turning to Hitcher, Burn walked to one of the emptied pelican cases and sat down.

"What Micky told me during the last call, we have about two more hours. Zapata is on his way, with twenty, maybe thirty trigger pullers backing him. Round numbers, guess work. We've got the place wired for the job, and it'll leave you and I doing some trigger work on the flunkies. Karma's going to deal with Zapata. Now's a good time to make peace if you need to."

"I'm good." Hitcher shrugged, "Never figured I'd make it this long. Was pretty sure I was done at Cleveland the first time. So, why are we letting Karma go one on one?"

"If we get the flunkies dealt with fast enough, we'll shift." Burn said, "But, of the three of us, she's got the best chance of handling him alone."

"She got some deep dark training or implants or something?"

"Nothing so mysterious." Burn shrugged, "It's more how she thinks. She's going to kill him, or die trying. And if she dies, she's going to die well."

"You good with that?"

"Were you good with your buddies going into battle during the war?"

"Nah, it always bothered me. I mean we were all big kids and we knew the score, but I never wanted them to actually get hurt or killed."

"Yeah, that's about how good I am with this." Burn said, "So, if Zapata kills her, you'll be on your own. Keep that in mind. But I don't know if it will come to that. Karma's one of the best I've seen with blades, guns or unarmed. That's not a fight to get in the middle of. She's committed."

"She's probably gonna win because she's right and on the side of justice?"

"No, she's committed to killing that dude. Whatever it takes. She might be justifying that she's protecting us, but she's just wired to commit or not do something. There's no reason to do something if you aren't committed to seeing it through to the end."

"Give me the phones. Grab your girl. Get the fuck out." Hitcher ground the words out, "I'll handle this."

"Too late. And, for the record, we'd probably lay you down, but Karma thinks that would put you off your game." Burn said, "Things are too tight to walk away. Besides, I learned a lot from Karma. I'm committed to seeing this through. It's what we do."

"No one listens to me," Hitcher said.

"Quit bitching. Never seen a guy want to kick out two hot chicks this badly before."

"Not many guys had death on two legs and a bunch of gunners coming his way." Hitcher said, "It's gonna be a funeral."

"If it is, lets' make sure the world knows we did something on the way out," Burn said.

"So, if we had twelve hours or so, you two would have gotten with me?" Hitcher asked.

"Shame we don't have time," Burn said, "But at least there's hope you'll get laid eventually."

Chapter 15

Karma watched all four camera feeds on the old laptop Micky's contacts had scrounged up. They ignored the source of the gear and weapons. Better to use them than be caught with them. Micky's intel indicated they would have plenty of opportunity to use everything.

She sat up when cars pulled up on the south and west facing camera. A moment later, more cars rolled up on the north and east cameras. Her hand dropped to the pistol in the drop holster on her leg. Another little gift Micky had come up with. She had a full load in her pistol, a grenade in a pouch on her belt, and her H&K. Her collection of knives confused Hitcher to the point that Karma silenced him in annoyance.

"Time to work," she said.

Burn tucked her rifle into her shoulder and glanced at Hitcher. He had his tactical rifle in a comfortable grip. His eyes were on the laptop, looking at the numbers coming out of the cars.

"This isn't going to be pretty."

"Or easy." Burn said, "Stay with me. And, whatever you do, don't shoot Karma."

"I'm not a big fan of friendly fire," Hitcher said.

"Neither are we." Burn said, "But there's no telling where she's going to pop up."

"Speaking of," Hitcher said, "Where did she go?"

A moment later, they heard feet across the roof of the office area they were occupying. Burn glanced up, tipping her chin.

"Like I said, check your targets." she said, "Let's get in position. North side. Zapata's coming in with the southern crew, so Karma gets them."

"And the traps should keep the east and west teams nervous and slow," Hitcher said.

"Yep. You want right or left side?"

"Lady's choice."

"You take right side," Burn said.

A sharp bang from the west side of the warehouse told them the hostiles had found a trap. Hitcher focused, watching the north entrance through the warehouse shelving. Burn leaned into the next shelving stand, rifle settled on the door. Both knew their cover sucked. Combined with the armor incorporated into their clothes, it was better than nothing. Another mine exploded on the west side.

"Working the hell out of that, aren't they?" Hitcher said.

"They do seem dedicated." Burn agreed, "Think he spent the cash to get better than average shooters?"

"Hope not." Hitcher said, "They're pushing our door open. Cautious types. Going slow, sweeping with a camera."

Burn fired through the door. The camera dropped.

"You're just being mean."

"Yes." Burn agreed, "Hope they get that message early."

Karma watched the team creep into the warehouse. They kept good cover over each other, scanning their sectors. Professionals. Zapata was distinct, his bald head reflecting the little light from the street lamps. If she got a chance to give the survivors a critique, she would mention that someone should have been tasked with checking 'up'.

She relaxed her grip on the grenade's safety spoon. The spoon went into a pocket of her jacket while she watched a timer display in her vision field count down from three seconds. She gently tossed the grenade, watching as it dropped into the middle of the formation. The team froze when they heard the metallic ping of the grenade bouncing off the concrete. It exploded half a second later. Zapata spun and crouched on the bounce, taking the fragments in the back of his jacket. He was blown to the door. His team was down, clutching at their legs. One reached for the leg that had been severed just below her knee.

Before they could react, Karma had the sub machine gun positioned and firing. Using bursts, she killed four before any of the team realized the threat. As they started pointing weapons randomly, Karma cat walked along the support beam. After several steps, she crouched again, bracing against the wall and a heavy support beam that ran to the ceiling.

Someone hit a tripwire from the east entrance. Two anti-personnel mines went off, one facing east, the other shredding two more of the south team. Taking a quick breath, Karma steadied her sights, and lit up another mercenary. Three troops and Zapata remained. Another burst, two left. Last burst. The one left started crawling for the door. Zapata came back into the warehouse, kicking the wounded mercenary. Karma finished the merc with a burst. Zapata spun, completing a full circle while Karma sat the sub machine gun on the shelf. When Zapata completed his circle, Karma dropped the three meters to the floor, letting her knees flex to take the impact. Her boots made just enough noise that Zapata froze.

"I'm back here," Karma said, "For such a great killer, you don't catch on fast."

"Fast enough to finish you, puta," Zapata spun, pistol spitting out tongues of flame as he turned.

"Gonna get pushed back," Hitcher fired another burst toward the half dozen troops forcing their way through the door.

"Works for me." Burn said, "Go right."

"Got it. Got a grenade?"

"Karma grabbed it. Have to make do with heavy fire."

"Better than the double barrel I ended up with during Cleveland Two," Hitcher said, firing a pair of bursts at a movement on his side. A scream rewarded his effort.

"Get to that story later. Cover north, I'll check our path."

"Got it," Hitcher fired at movement. Burn turned, rifle barrel high as she passed him.

"We good?" Hitcher asked after a second.

"Hold what you got. They're at the office."

"Tell me when to duck," Hitcher chuckled.

"Opening the door, duck now."

Hitcher crouched, watching the north end of the warehouse. The team that entered from that side knew to stay low, but they had to move into the debris filled walk ways to get close to their quarry. One of them crept around a shelf stack, staying close to the shelves. Hitcher fired two rounds and watched the man drop.

Noise and heat washed up his back. The concussion from the pair of anti-personnel mines going off slammed him into a shelf support. Screams came from the mercenaries caught in the cross blasts of the mines, one mounted to fill the opened door, and the second outside, to clear through the open areas of shelving. Burn fired a few bursts. Her magazine clattered on the floor.

"Mother fucker." he grunted, "You good?"

"Moving on three. Outside wall and move south."

"Go," Hitcher agreed.

On her three, they both moved. Hitcher fired a magazine to keep the surviving members of the north team pinned down, while Burn was delivering the same treatment to the west team. They had been hammered by the double mine trap, so there was little fight left.

"Ammo? This no comms shit sucks."

"Down one magazine," Hitcher replied, "half through the second one."

"I'm down two. Grab from the cache as we go by and watch the north end. I'll lead south. We should be able to move on the east team from the door."

Another mine, muffled by the walls of the office, exploded. Smoke billowed through the warehouse as debris burned. Wounded screamed, shots were fired apparently at whatever shadows happened to move in front the mercenaries.

"Not heavily modded," Hitcher said, "Not sure if that's good or bad."

"Bad. Bullets from random shooters kill you just as dead as aimed rounds to the head. Fuck. Going low light. Too much fire for thermographic."

"Movement north," Hitcher fired once. His target thudded against the floor.

"He was wearing a helmet." Hitcher said as he caught Burn's look, "You see Karma?"

"No, but I can hear metal on metal, so she's still alive."

"East team next?"

"Yeah, just fire up survivors as we pass. Sounds like they set off the other side already. Door's open."

"Let's move," Hitcher said.

They angled to the office area. Burn checked through the shattered windows. Hitcher shifted to the corner, scanning to the north. A fast burst put a head down farther up the corridor. Only a few people tried to return fire from the north, their shots hitting walls and shelves.

"Which way?" Hitcher looked for his next target.

"South side," Burn said, "Might see Karma and keeps something between us and those assholes."

"Tap me when you're ready," Hitcher said. The white dot settled on what looked like the side of a head peeking out from a distant shelving post. He fired a single shot, and the head shape snapped back.

"Nice shot." Burn tapped his shoulder, "Moving!"

Rising to his feet, Hitcher stepped backward, letting his cybereyes cycle through several visual spectrum while he listened to Burn's steps, trying to match her speed. He was off but close enough. During the war, he and his guys could move through unknown areas in total darkness without speaking and never lose distance and position. This was his first time operating tactically with Burn, so he did not expect such perfection.

"Turning right," Burn called.

He heard the shift in her steps. Burn gasped.

"What?" he asked.

"Karma."

Chapter 16

Their pistols had emptied out long before. His had been tossed across the floor. He had a nasty tear along his cheek from where Karma had caught him with her hot barrel. Blood soaked into the arm of her jacket sleeve, the price she paid for blocking his response to that. Since then, they had traded a few small nicks, but no serious wounds.

"Little puta." Zapata said, "You're brave, at least. Do you want to die first or hear your friends before I finish you?"

"Not going to be a concern," Karma blocked another knife thrust with her blade.

"So confident. Foolish, but confident." Zapata said, slashing at her, "I think I will let you listen. First the thief. Then your partner."

Karma slashed, getting a long gash up Zapata's blocking arm. She followed up with a sharp punch to the shoulder of his knife hand. Twisting in, she caught his armored jacket with the tip of her knife. Fabric tore, but the armor held as she danced out of his reach.

"You should call for help," Karma said, "Because you aren't good enough for that."

"You think that's something, puta?" Zapata grinned, "I'm gonna put your little knife somewhere you won't like."

"Promises, promises. Don't make 'em if you can't keep 'em."

He came in, stabbing fast at Karma. She blocked, trusting the fibers woven through her muscles to compensate for his mass. It worked, and her reflexes allowed her to redirect his attacks. His advantage in mass would eventually wear her down. He was showing no sign of slowing his assault. Finally, he managed to connect with a punch from his free hand.

Karma had dermal layers implanted under her skin to prevent injuries from blows, bullets or punctures. Like any armor, it was not perfect. Stars shot through her vision from the impact. She spun with the blow, pushed off a steel riser. Using the energy, she dropped low, letting her foot snap out in a spinning kick. Hooking his leg, she drove through with all the force she had.

Zapata's body twisted. He was an experienced fighter, though. He rolled with the energy, tucked and came back to his feet, getting the knife between them as he rose. She had bought some distance and a heartbeat to recover with the kick. Both of them gasped in ragged breaths as they circled, closing the gap.

"Do you think little things will get you through this, puta?" Zapata said, focusing on her as he shifted in.

"You get by well enough with little things." Karma replied, "Cabron."

"I'll let your girlfriend keep her tongue so she can tell you about little things when I'm fucking her," Zapata snapped, feinting a stab.

Karma let the bait pass, easing in a few more centimeters to close the gap.

"You got a real problem with women, carbon." she said, "Was madre mean to you? Did she make you eat your Brussels sprouts?"

"I got no problem with women, puta." he said, "A stupid cusca who thinks she can stand up to a man? That problem I handle."

"Remember that," Karma said, "during what comes next."

"Listening to you scream and beg? I'll remind -"

Karma moved, her massively augmented system pushing her body hard. Seeing her coming, Zapata slashed his blade out. He saw that he was too slow, she ducked under the blade, losing a few strands of hair. Bright pain flashed from his leg and then he felt her other arm around his neck, her fingers gouging the skin on his head. More pain erupted as something moved in his thigh.

"Good thing I'm not a stupid cusca." Karma whispered, "I'll give your head to your masters. So they remember I'm not to be trifled with."

He tried to find some heat, some rage to strike out at her with. His vision clouded, and it seemed suddenly cold, despite his exertion. Sinking to his knees, he tried to speak, but his mouth and tongue seemed thick, unable to move.

"If we meet again, cabron, it'll be in hell. If I meet you there, I'll take your cock, just so the demons know you're my bitch," Karma said, easing him to the concrete floor. His knife rolled out of his limp hand.

"Well, fuck," Karma looked down. He had managed to cut a long gash down her leg, "Gonna need some good nanos for that."

"Mother fuck," Hitcher said.

A burst of shots got his attention back on the job. Burn rushed forward, rifle up. When she fired again, another burst, the rifle barely moved. Hitcher closed the distance, keeping his rifle level.

"You get to the corner, I'll cover right."

"Cool." Burn said, "What about left?"

"Your girl has that."

"Point." Burn swept her rifle across the shelving, "Go right."

Hitcher made the turn, sweeping the path ahead. Smoke thickened from the fires burning in the office space drifting through the shattered windows. He tried to breath as shallowly as he could while he let his eyes shift. Someone cut the corner around a shelf and into the corridor. Thought never entered into the matter. The trigger went back, a trio of hot casings jangled into the office area, and the body jerked, stood for half a heartbeat, and then dropped to the floor. As he had done so many times during the war, Hitcher moved past the corpse.

Hitcher's next problem area was the office's corner. Hostiles might be waiting around it. Even if they were not, it provided them some cover. Old experience came forward and Hitcher kept a steady pace. He closed on the corner, shifted the muzzle of his rifle to the extreme left and swept it steadily back, checking every shadow for any kind of heat signature.

At the corner, he finished his sweep with the rifle aimed low and down as he turned. It was two meters to reach the next corridor. Another shooter rounded that corner, a pistol rising in his hands. Hitcher knew the odds, the research, the training.

According to all the data, there was no way, baring extensive levels of reflex modification systems or biological enhancers, that he might shoot first.

It had happened numerous times during the war. Hitcher kept the muzzle moving, watching the caret in his field of vision sweep across. He felt the first hit against his thigh. There was no burning sensation, so he trusted the armored pants to handle the hit. The caret came closer. Another sharp thud against his ribs. The caret reached the target's chest. Hitcher fired a single shot.

The shooter fired a third round into the window a few centimeters to Hitcher's right. Hitcher's second shot was center mass, right over the target's heart. Riding the recoil through, Hitcher fired again as the caret settled. His target collapsed, balling up as he settled to the floor. Moving close, Hitcher kicked the pistol away. He heard two more bursts from where Burn should have been. Without their communications systems, he had no way to know whether it was Burn shooting or being shot at. It passed idly through his mind that both could be possible. He stepped past the brains and blood spreading from the dead man's ruined head.

Shaking off the thought, he pushed toward the north wall. Random items on the shelves blurred by as he trotted the remaining distance to the end of the shelves. Someone fired off half a dozen shots. One sparked off the floor at the end of the shelving. Without conscious thought, Hitcher moved, turning right as he went wide around the corner. The shooter was at the far corner of the building, fumbling his reload.

Hitcher felt the recoil, watched the hot flashes as they impacted the shooter's body. The magazine slid out of the shooter's hand. His empty pistol clattered to the concrete. Dropping to his knees, his head lowered and vomit spewed across the concrete.

As the target finally fell forward, Hitcher swept the area until he was facing the opposite wall, and then swept back. The man was still down. A few long steps brought Hitcher to the corner. One boot on the man's back confirmed the target stayed down, while he checked the path behind him again, and then to the south. Near the eastern door, Burn leaned against the wall, her rifle resting in one hand. She gave him a thumbs up.

"Clear," he called out.

"Clear," she agreed, her eyes continuing to sweep the factory.

"Clear south." Karma called, "Anyone who's not us, get the fuck out!"

"You okay?" Hitcher called to Karma.

"I'm good. See if you can find a shovel or something. This will take all damn night, otherwise. Told you I'd fight and fuck him."

Chapter 17

"Micky said he'd have a silver platter when we get back," Burn said.

A trio watched them in the basement room. Hitcher had already changed clothes. Even in the poor lighting, he looked a lot more like a heavy laborer than the combat shooter they had seen hours before.

"Cool." Karma said, "You guys got our boy?"

"We got him." the man said. No names had been exchanged, "He's got a lot to learn, and he'll have time while we wait for the cops to calm down about that factory."

"Cool." Karma said, again, "We need to hole up or head out?"

"I'd be happier hiding just him." The man said, "So far, it looks like they think it was a gang thing. Probably a drug deal gone south. Some guy missing a head is almost always Hispanic or Asian gang action here."

"The guy who did that was really pissed off," Karma said.

"Yeah. We're getting rid of your ride, since it's come up on the stolen vehicle reports," the man said, "We've got you another car. Sell it to a chop shop when you get out."

"Will do." Burn said, "Assume if we're caught with it, we'll get the hit for something nasty?"

"Good assumption. Common car, hacked registration, and changed the paint. Plus, it's a bonus for us if that particular nasty remains unsolved. Any problem with that?"

"As long as you aren't setting us up. Understand that if you are, sooner or later, I'll be along to settle up with you."

"Never pays to cross up good operators. And Micky thinks you two are good assets. Plus, we got a few lines on the Empire's operations up here thanks to your little action. So, no, not setting you up."

"Where's our ride?" Burn asked.

"On the way. You've got about five minutes."

"So, Hitcher, you sure about this?" Burn asked.

"Yeah, I'm sure. Pays okay, I'll be doing good work, and the scenery does not stay the same."

"Alright. You change your mind, give us a call," Burn said.

"For a fee, we'll be happy to get you back home," Karma agreed.
"I think that might be a compliment," Hitcher grinned.

"There are people she's demanded a fee to speak to," Burn said, "So, yeah, if my girl is willing to work for you, it is."

"Time for a hug?" Hitcher asked.

Burn and Karma came in and hugged him with a fierceness that surprised Hitcher. Finally, after enough time that the observers started shuffling uncomfortably, they ended the embrace. When they let him go, they smiled.

Burn punched Hitcher in the arm. He knew she had pulled the punch, but it was still faster and harder than he thought she could hit.

"Told you I'd punch you for making Karma grin."

"Your ride is pulling up," the man said.

"Later, Hitcher," Burn said.

"Don't get shot." Karma said, "Getting shot sucks."

"Been there," Hitcher agreed, "Go easy on the knife fights."

"Not likely," Karma said, grabbing the heavy duffel bag with the ends of thick plastic sticking up out of it.

"Didn't figure." Hitcher said, "Roll smart and shoot straight."

"Always." Burn said, "Stay low and move quick."

The others lead Burn and Karma up to the street. A nondescript man was walking away from the blue sedan running on the curb as they stepped out. Karma headed for the driver's side, tossing her bags on the rear seat, while Burn opened the passenger door and dropped in. Settling in behind the controls, Karma looked the instruments over. With a grin, she set the radio to take auxiliary audio feed. A moment later, she had an old metal band's song coming over the speakers. Burn turned it down to the point she would not have to scream.

"You good?"

"Wireless feed, cruise control, the auto drive is disabled, and full of fuel." Karma said, "Next stop, Cincinnati."

"Cincinnati?"

"Canoli. I only got to eat like four. We're technically still working until we get home, so I want my share."

"Fair enough," Burn said.

"You ever turn Hitcher's comms back on?"

"They'll sync up in an hour or so. I left him a present, though."

"Oh?"

"Remember that picture of us after the party in Marietta?"

"That's just mean, Burn," Karma said.

"Somehow, I doubt he'll agree with you."

"Turn the radio up. I need driving music and coffee until we get canoli."

"Drive on, hon." Burn said, pressing the volume up button, "We've got one more easy job when we get home."

Epilogue

Jason Cordova had just completed his training as an analyst for the Central Intelligence Agency. He had a few thoughts about that as he looked over his cube. No note pads, no printer, no sticky pads, nothing to take notes with. His implanted phone was shut down in the facility. On the one hand, he was glad that intelligence training from the Army was useful, and that he still held a security clearance. On the other, he was happy to have full time employment and decent benefits. Health insurance had been murder in the private sector.

He started his second day by sitting his employer provided coffee mug on the counter and logged onto his system. Within a few minutes, he faced at the icons on the display. First, he opened his email, since that was the primary communications tool for the agency. Next, he opened the folder showing the items he needed to process.

Scrolling through his email gave him a few minutes. Nothing spectacular, just notes on upcoming 'system improvement' dates and schedules, which would glitch up the programs and bog down the network even more, according to the old hands in the office. It had taken Jason about three hours the previous day to understand that no one was working there to be happy or patriotic. They were there because the work was steady and paid on time.

After sorting his emails, and deleting numerous pointless messages, he switched to the processing folder. A dozen images of random vehicles at check points came up. He sent those to vehicle processing, since there were no easily visible faces in the images and the system had already flagged them as 'ones', the lowest threat level. A couple of people came up, rated one to three. Jason did not question where the people came from or what they were doing. Rather, he guessed where to send the images based on the priority for further investigation.

Next he got an image of two women walking out of a convenience store with coffee. The image was tagged as a level two priority. Therefore they were not horribly dangerous. Something about it twigged Jason's memory, so he double clicked on the image. Analysts were allowed to give further examination, as long as they did not spend much time on it. As a new hire, his job was to get intelligence hits to someone more experienced to investigate.

This was not a huge threat feeling, though. Jason examined the women for a few seconds and realized that the blond was familiar. Someone he had seen before, long ago. No particular good or bad feelings involved, and no hint that he had seen her during the war.

It finally settled. He was pretty sure she was the pretty girl he remembered sharing the long bus ride from Denver to Chicago with when he had joined the Army. She had been heading to Chicago for a change and a chance to start over.

At least, she looked like that girl. More than a decade has passed since that bus ride, Jason realized. Finally, he sent the image to the next group to wade through. Another sip of coffee and a glance at the clock on the monitor. He had an hour and a half to go before his first scheduled break. After rubbing his eyes, he started into the next group of images.